I Can Read! ™ SHARED My First READING

THIS **Pete the Cat**
COLLECTION BELONGS TO:

_____

Dear Parent:
Your child's love of reading starts here!

Every child learns to read in a different way and at his or her own speed. Some go back and forth between reading levels and read favorite books again and again. Others read through each level in order. You can help your young reader improve and become more confident by encouraging his or her own interests and abilities. From books your child reads with you to the first books he or she reads alone, there are I Can Read Books for every stage of reading:

SHARED READING
Basic language, word repetition, and whimsical illustrations, ideal for sharing with your emergent reader

BEGINNING READING
Short sentences, familiar words, and simple concepts for children eager to read on their own

READING WITH HELP
Engaging stories, longer sentences, and language play for developing readers

READING ALONE
Complex plots, challenging vocabulary, and high-interest topics for the independent reader

ADVANCED READING
Short paragraphs, chapters, and exciting themes for the perfect bridge to chapter books

I Can Read Books have introduced children to the joy of reading since 1957. Featuring award-winning authors and illustrators and a fabulous cast of beloved characters, I Can Read Books set the standard for beginning readers.

A lifetime of discovery begins with the magical words **"I Can Read!"**

*Visit www.icanread.com for information
on enriching your child's reading experience.*

ISBN: 978-0-06-285953-2

18 19 20 21 22 SCP 10 9 8 7 6 5 4 3 2 1

First Edition

Kohl's
Style number: 9780062859532
Factory Number 123386
05/2018

Pete the Cat

I Can Read!

SHARED My First READING

PETE'S BIG LUNCH

By James Dean

MAYO

BREAD

3 TREASURED STORYBOOKS for Young Readers!

Pete the Cat

AND THE SURPRISE TEACHER

HELLO MY NAME IS

by James Dean

Pete the Cat's

TRAIN TRIP

CAT

by James Dean

HARPER

An imprint of HarperCollinsPublishers

TABLE OF CONTENTS

Pete the Cat

PETE'S BIG LUNCH

by James Dean

Here comes Pete!

It is lunchtime.
Pete is ready to eat.

What should Pete eat?

A sandwich would be nice.

Yes, Pete wants a sandwich.
Pete opens the fridge.

He takes out a loaf of bread.
He finds a yummy fish.

He adds tomato and mayo.

Pete looks at his sandwich.
It is too small.
Something is missing.

Pete knows what it needs.

His sandwich needs an apple.

Pete loves apples!

His sandwich needs crackers.
Crackers are crunchy.
Pete loves crunchy crackers!

Pete looks at his sandwich again.
It is still too small.

Pete is very hungry.

Pete adds a pickle.

Pete adds cheese.

Pete adds an egg,

two hot dogs,

a banana,

and a can of beans.

Something is missing.

Pete adds ice cream!
He takes three huge scoops.

Pete's sandwich
is too big
for Pete to eat.

Pete wonders
what to do.
Pete thinks
and thinks.

"I've got it!" Pete says.
Pete calls all of his friends.

He asks them to come over.

Everyone goes to Pete's house.
They are all very hungry.

Pete shows them
his big lunch.

"Are you hungry?" asks Pete.
Pete's sandwich is big enough
for everyone.
"Dig in!" says Pete.

Pete's sandwich is good.

Pete's sandwich is VERY good.

Pete's sandwich is all gone.
Pete's friends are full.
They liked Pete's big lunch.

"Thanks for lunch,"
Pete's friends say.
"Thanks for sharing!"

"You're welcome," Pete says.
Sharing is cool.

Pete the Cat

AND THE SURPRISE TEACHER

HELLO MY NAME IS

by James Dean

Pete is ready for school.
"Where is Mom?" Pete asks.

"She has a surprise for you,"
says Pete's dad.

Pete goes to school.
His mom is there.
What a surprise!

"Hi, class. I am Mrs. Cat,"
says Pete's mom.
"I am the substitute teacher."

"I will need your help today,"
says Pete's mom.
"What do we do first?"

"Art!" says Pete.
"Yeah!" says the class.

The class lines up.
Pete's mom leads the line.

"Is this art?" asks Pete's mom.

Boing!
This is not art.

This is gym.
"Stay and play!"
says the gym teacher.

The class plays.
"Gym is fun with more kids!"
says Pete.

Gym is over.
Pete's mom takes
the class to art.

MUSIC

La, la, la!
This is not art.

This is music.
"Stay and sing!"
says the music teacher.

The class sings.
"We are louder with
more kids!" says Pete.

Rumble!
Pete is hungry.
Time for lunch!

This is not the
lunchroom.

This is the playground!
"Let's have a picnic,"
says Pete.

"Now it is time
for art," says Pete's mom.
Everyone cheers.

Pete leads the class.
"Is this art?"
asks Pete's mom.

It is!
Lots of kids are
making art.

58

"Oh no," says the art teacher.
"It is too late to join us.
The day is almost over."

The class goes to
their classroom.
"I know!" says Pete.

"Let's make art here!"
he says.
"Okay," says Pete's mom.

Pete calls a huddle.
Whisper, whisper.
The class plans a surprise.

Pete draws.
Callie makes paper cats.
Everyone helps.

"Surprise!" says Pete.
The class made art for
Pete's mom!

"Thank you, Mrs. Cat!"
says the class. "We had a
great day with you!"

Sometimes a different day
is an awesome day!

Pete the Cat's
TRAIN TRIP

by
James Dean

Pete the Cat is going
to visit his grandma.
He gets to ride on a train!

Pete's mom buys three tickets.
She gives one to Pete
and one to his brother, Bob.

Pete looks up at the big board.
"Our train is leaving at
ten o'clock," he says.

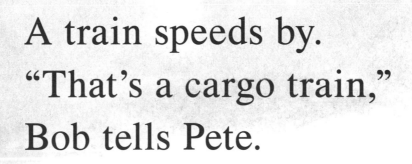

A train speeds by.
"That's a cargo train,"
Bob tells Pete.

71

Pete's train has arrived.
"All aboard!"
calls the conductor.

Pete's mom finds three seats.
"I can't wait to see Grandma,"
says Bob.

"I can't wait to explore
the train!" says Pete.

The conductor comes
to collect the tickets.
Pete hands over his.

"I love trains," says Pete.
"I'll show you around,"
says the conductor.

Pete follows the conductor
from car to car as the floor
rumbles under his feet.

"Wow!" Pete says when they get to the caboose.
"We're going over a bridge."

Pete sees his mom and Bob.
They are at the snack bar!

"I got this for you," says Bob.

Pete follows the conductor.
He goes to the front of the train.

"Come in!" says the engineer.

"Wow!" Pete says.
The engineer shows him
the engine.

The engineer shows Pete
the train's brakes.
There is a tunnel up ahead!

As they go through the tunnel,
Pete gets to honk the horn.
Toot! Toot!

Everything is light again!
"Thanks for showing
me around," Pete says.

On his way back to his seat,
Pete stops and makes
new friends.

They live in different towns.
They are getting off
at different stops.

Pete plays games.
A little kid wears his hat.
Pete sings a song.

What a groovy ride!

"We get off at the next stop," says Pete's mom.

Toot! Toot!

Pete looks out the window
and sees . . .

"Grandma!"

Pete is the first one
off the train.

Pete's grandma gives him
a big hug.
It feels good.

Pete loves riding the train.
But he loves his grandma
even more!